HOCKEY

HUMOR

By
Charles Hellman and Robert Tiritilli

I0571331

Hockey Cover

TIRITILLI

ISBN 9780935938470
Illustrations by Robert A. Tiritilli
Cover & Interior Design by Charles S. Hellman
Edited by Charles S. Hellman

Cartoonist - Robert A. Tiritilli

With years of strong draftsman skills, Robert Tiritilli helped create his outlandish style and talent of sports cartooning by dually employing representative portraiture, and cartoonish lightheartedness.

Hockey Review

There is a point in the life of every novice and aficionado hockey fan when cartoons based on wordplay and images that are hysterically funny. This humor book is for those who are at that joyous stage in life.

Ice hockey is a contact team sport played on ice, usually in a rink, in which two teams of skaters use their sticks to shoot a vulcanized rubber puck into their opponent's net to score points. The sport is known to be fast-paced and physical, with teams usually consisting of six players each: one goaltender, and five players who skate up and down the ice trying to take the puck and score a goal against the opposing team. Perhaps no sport has more words, terms and phrases that lend themselves to humorous reinterpretation based on their literal meaning than hockey. Ice hockey is believed to have evolved from simple stick and ball games played in the 18th and 19th century United Kingdom and elsewhere.

Charles S. Hellman and Robert A. Tiritilli have clearly kept their ability to look at the world through ingenuous eyes, and we are the beneficiaries of their vision. This hockey humor book contains over 100 one-paneled, pen and ink drawings that are reproduced in black and white except on the front and back cover of this soft cover book.

In the cartoon of a hockey player carrying all his belongings is being charged for icing. Icing is an infraction in the sport of ice hockey. It occurs when a player shoots the puck from behind the centre red line, across the opposing team's goal line, and the puck remains untouched.

Some cartoons are not nearly so clever. Can you imagine the one for "Break-away"? Your guess won't be far off the mark. But in some cases, the cartoons take the obvious humor and make it better with a hilarious execution.

These cartoons will tickle your funny bone. Novices, however, will have a few of the cartoons explained to them (as employing hockey terms they may not know such as "Wraparound"). From the novice's point of view, this will be only a four-star book because it doesn't have color inside.

If you are knowledgeable to figure out the "Bench Warmer" cartoon without explanation, this hockey cartoon book could be a good gift.

Hockey 101

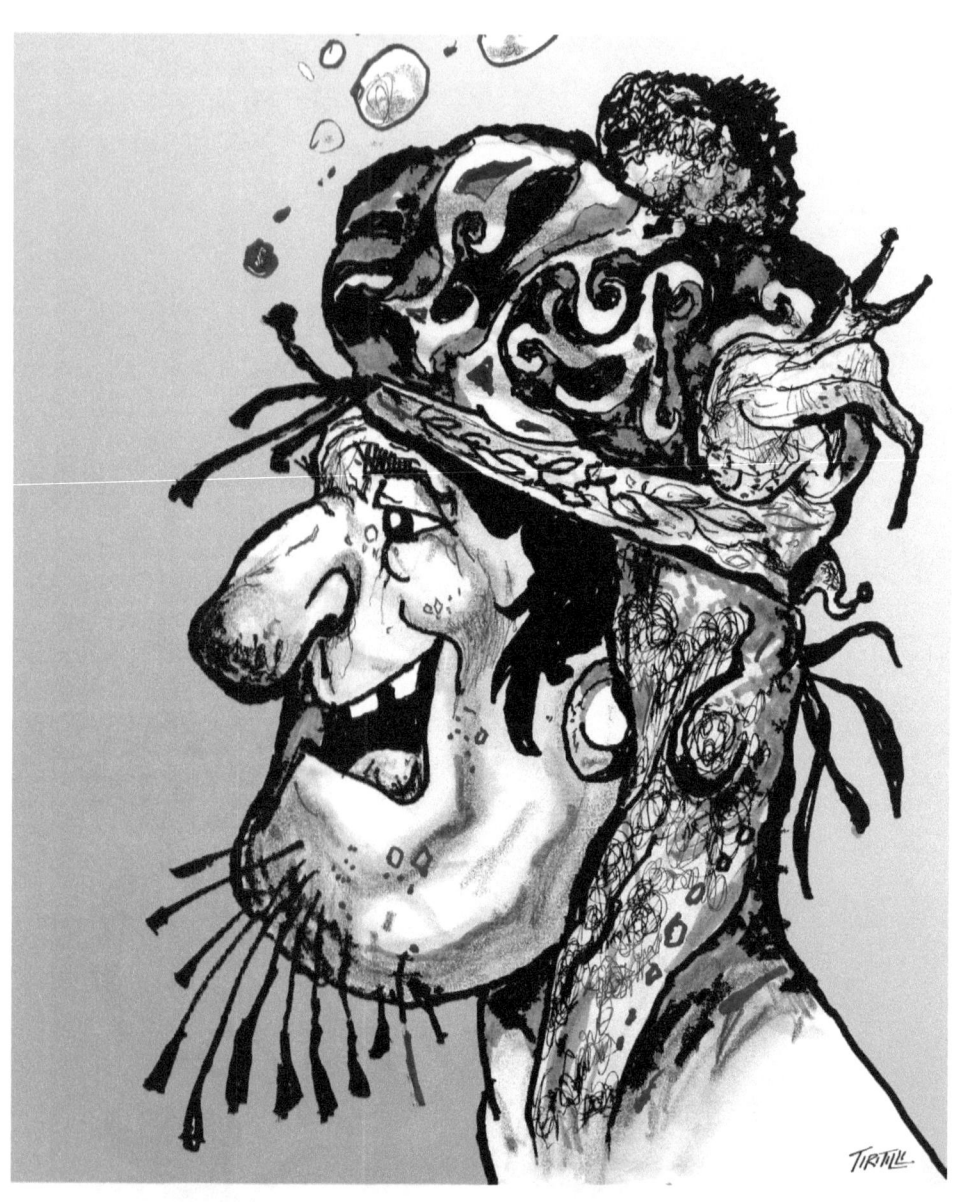

Hockey is a fast body-contact game played on ice by men with sticks in their hands and skate on knives laced to their shoes.

Referees initiate the
GET TOUGH POLICY

Ultimate "FACE OFF"

"I hockey befriend you!"

"Let's play agua-hockey!"

**"No! I am NOT
one of those ugly ducklings!"**

**It doesn't matter if you win or lose,
until you lose!**

Our hockey team never wins!
But we are entertaining!

"Oh swami!
Should I bet on our home hockey team
or the visiting team?"

Sports nut

Hockey Mom

Ooogg invents First Hockey Puck

I never claimed ice hockey players
could walk on water.

"Our mascot was hungry."

"That's FAKE NEWS!"

"I don't write FAKE NEWS!"

**"What do you mean...
my food stamps aren't excepted here."**

"Did you know...
most hockey players are bilingual?"
"Yeah... they know English and profanity."

Hell's Hockey TV Room

Hockey fans

More Hockey fans

**Exercise can't kill you...
but why take the chance?**

"You didn't meet your hockey goals!"
"Not to worry, we'll just set new ones."

"So you played three years at
"Sing Sing".
That doesn't strike a cord with me!"

"I know... let's play him near the net!"

He took the last shot.

Jacques gets called for ICING.

**"I have nothing to say about hockey...
and I'll say it only once!"**

Breakaway

"Professor, is it Ancient Hockey?"

Bench Warmer

Coach mixes up the slides.

**One of our worst fears...
nothing to snack on.**

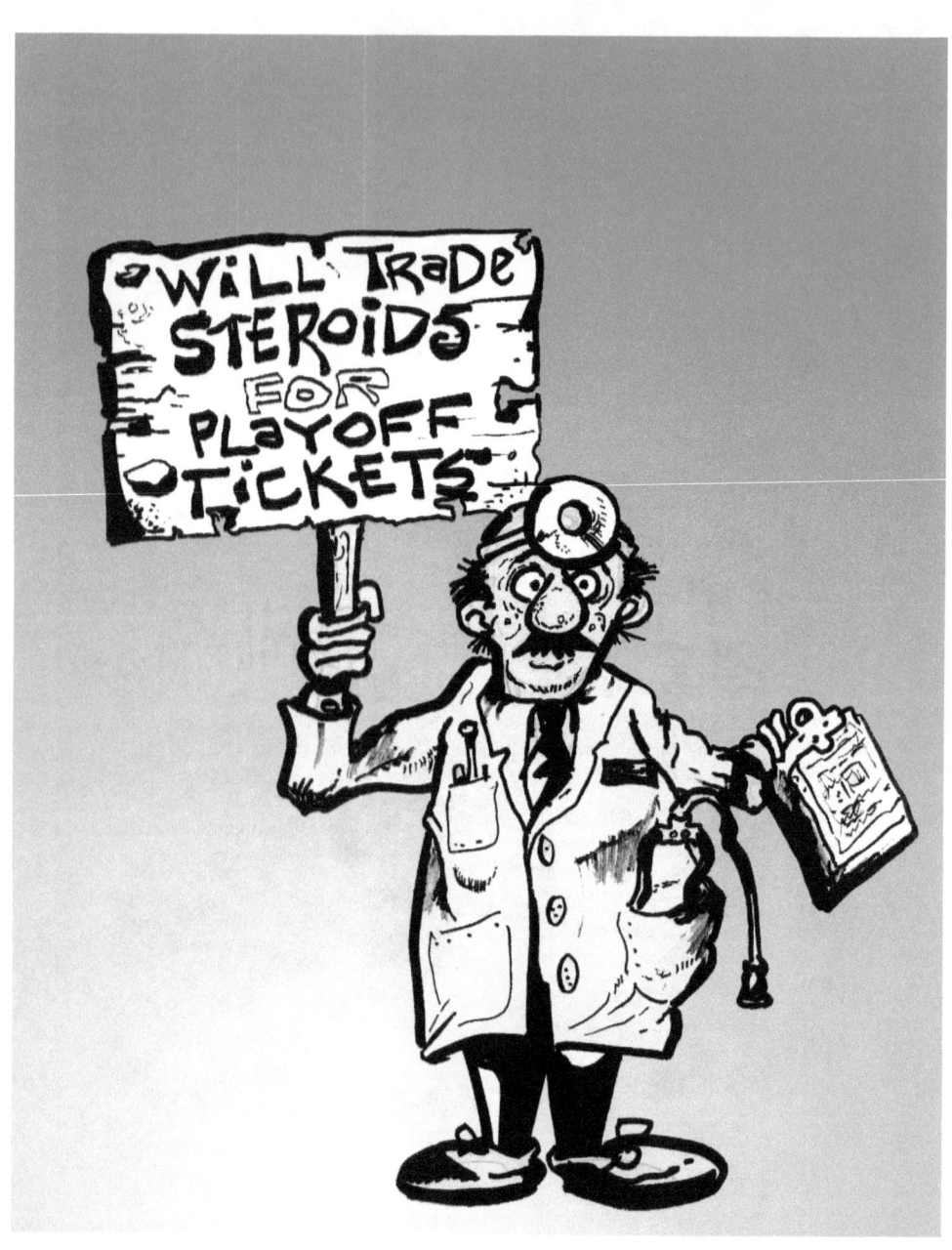

Sub

Hard nose

"Personally, I prefer the name
*Land Tunas.***"**

"Our mascot was hungry."

**"I always thought hockey
was a non-violent sport."**

Important hockey meeting
with management

Riding the pine

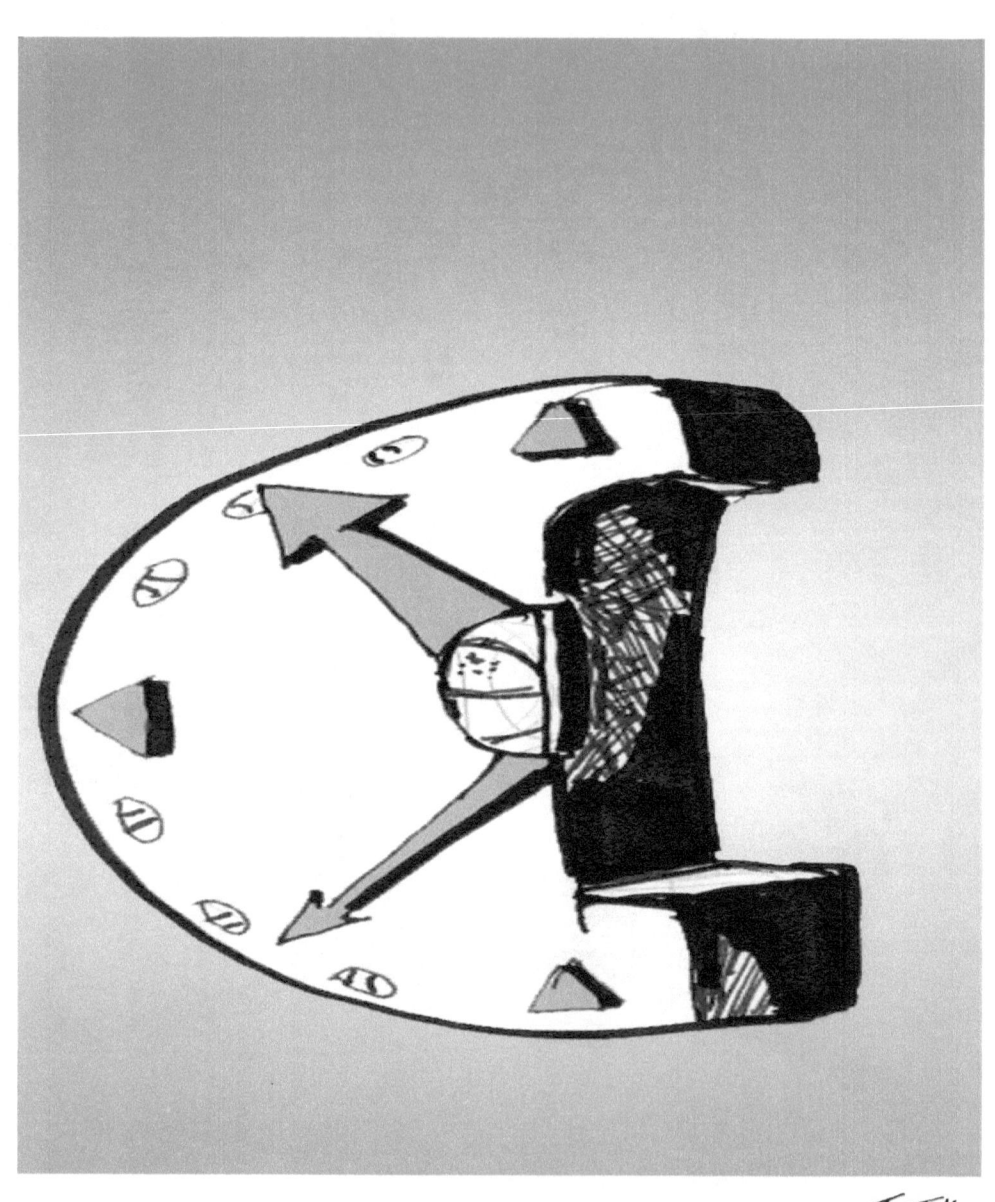

Half-Time

Referee

**"Why do they call you...
BIG DOG?"**

"Professor,
hockey players don't understand
Quantum Physics."

"I don't think you are ready for the NHL."

**Dr. Malet invents the sport concussion...
brings problem to a head!**

**"I think you missed placed
a decimal point somewhere."**

**"My hockey team is from Canada...
I think!"**

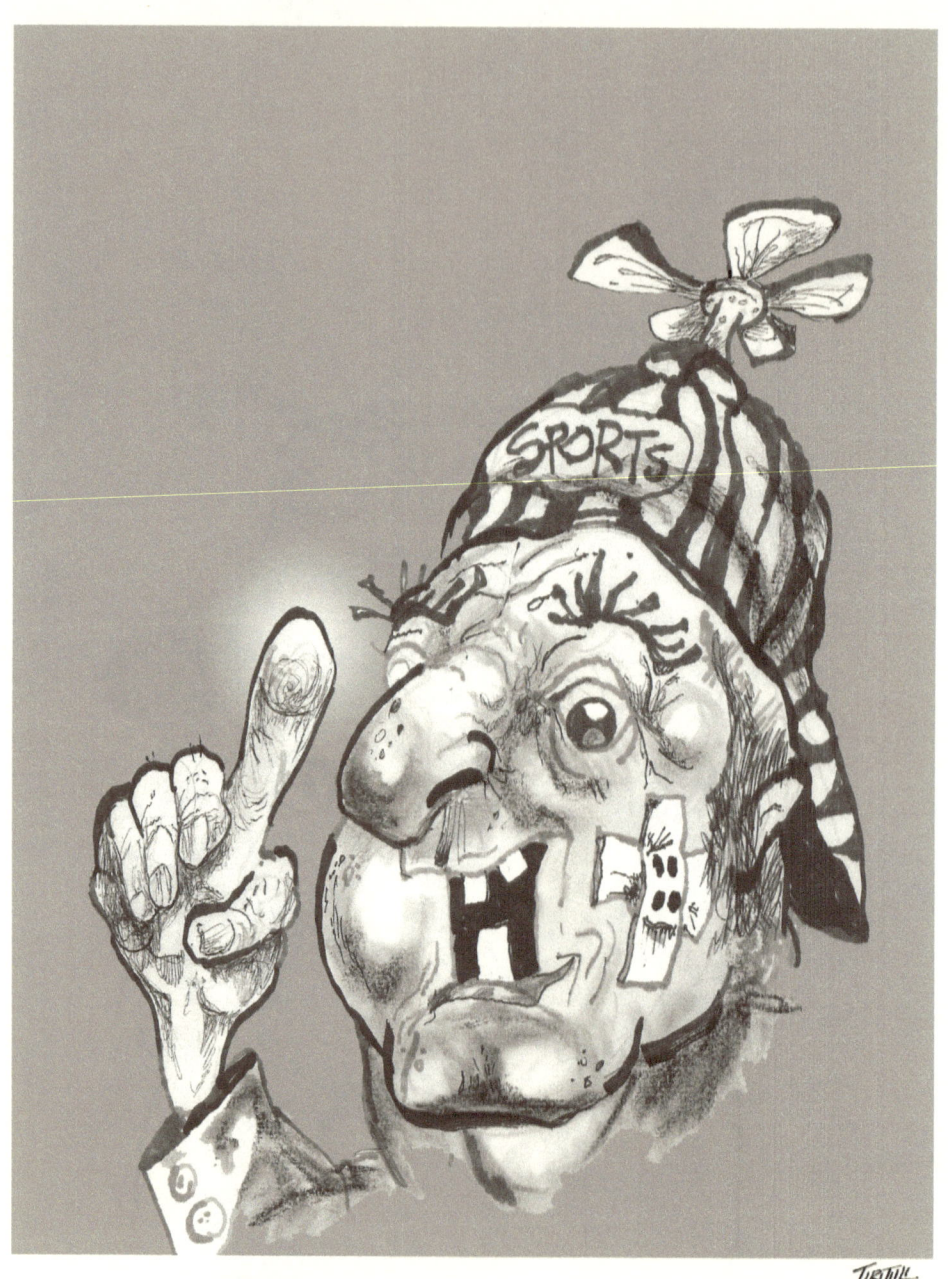

**"Who ever said hockey
is a non-contact sport... was wrong!"**

**"You should have seen
the shot I made from the blue line!**

**"Raise your right hand
if you were drafted by a NHL team."**

**Alexander Graham Bell
invents the *CELL phone*...
becomes the first sports telemarker!**

"My concussion beats yours all to hell!"

"He's got WiFi!"

"Look Mom! I just signed up to play. And I got this humongous trophy!"

Millennials call home!

Fan's fan

"Is this your hockey team mascot's idea of *Meet & Greet*?"

"My team fired me for being a chicken...
they said the egg came first!"

"Which tribe do you belong to?"

"Honey, I sold our playoff hockey seats for two weeks in Hawaii!"

The face of the NHL

"... and who wants to play in the NHL?"

"Sign here... I know you would make a great hockey player!"

"Maybe less exercise will help!"

**Hockey and reality leave
a lot to the imagination!**

**"You don't have Mad Cow's disease...
you have Sports Frenzy."**

"The difference was he was low-sticking
and you were high-sticking!"

"It's a computer game that allows you a little life between your kids' hockey games and practices."

The evolution of a hockey player

"We traded you for him."

"You hockey players sure get sensitive with these prostate exams."

**"Congratulations *LUCKY*!
They awarded you the *game puck*."**

Numnick's mother was so happy he won a gold medal that she had it bronzed.

Athlete's foot

**Sport losers are doomed
to the rath of HELL's BELLS!**

**BIG FOOTS gather to honor
their first brand sports skate.**

FREE HOTDOGS!

**"Nobody in hockey
should be considered a genius.
A genius is a guy like Ezra Einstein!"**

**"I used to play for
the Reindeers' hockey team!"**

**"Please, try not to hurt any of them,
they're your hockey teammates!"**

"I always keep a picture of my hockey agent on my locker so I can fine my clothes!"

At Hockey Officals Rehab Camp

"You can play hockey or checkers!"

"Raise your hand, if you were on the hockey team last year."

"There is no "EYE" in team!"

**"Big Foot" meets "Big Foot"
before their EPIC hockey game!**

**"Motivation, HELL!
It just puts them to sleep."**

**"It take a lot of hockey team violence
to finally get him to smile!"**

"I promote those second string
hockey players to the 1st team because
they've been here a while."

**"Yeti, Sasquatch, Big Foot,
to be scarier...
I changed my name to 401K!"**

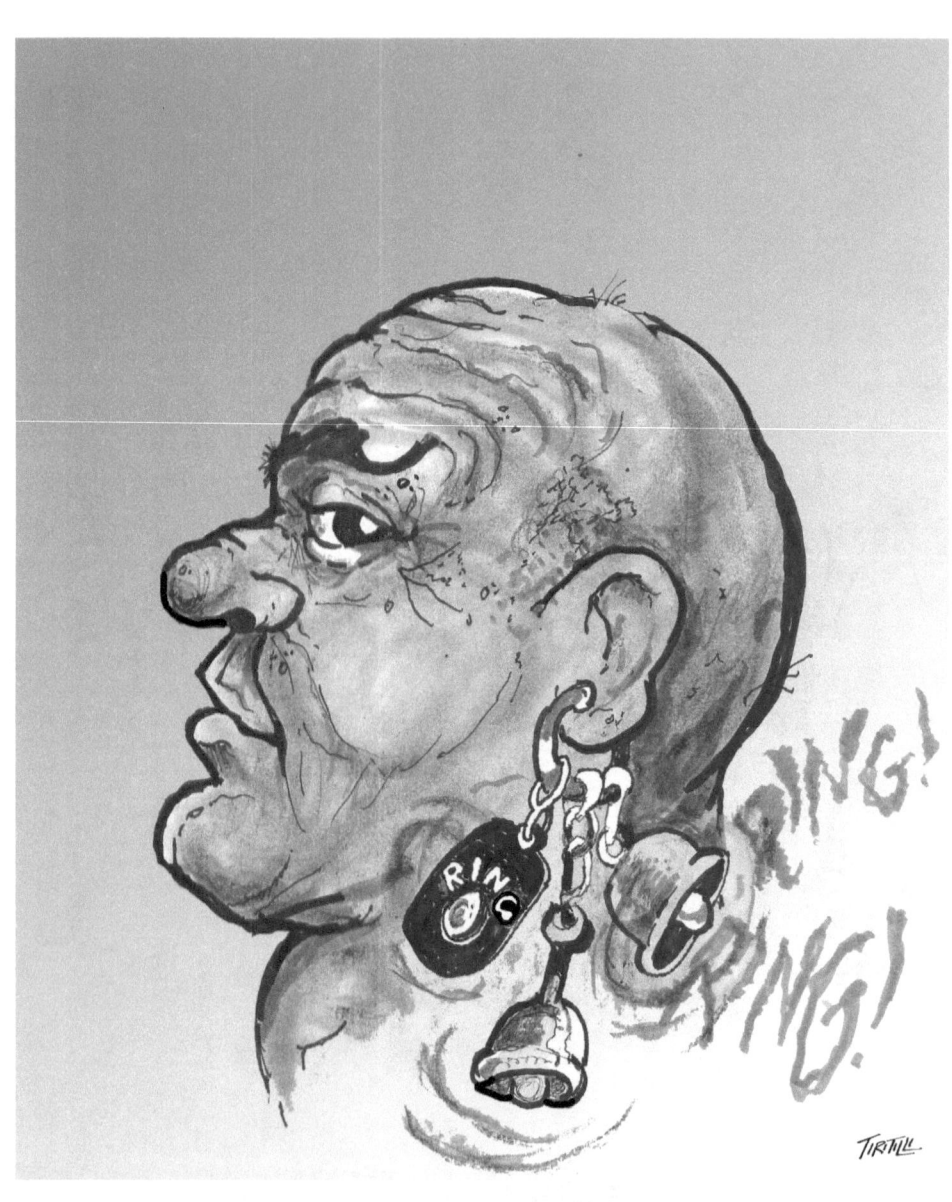

**Real hockey players
wear earRINGS!**

"I'm not perfect,
but I'm perfect for your hockey team."

"I start exercising at six o'clock in the morning NO MATTER what time is."

"I'm going to graduate on time
NO matter how long it takes!"

"Don't fret! You're just like Einstein. He got D's in college. He also got F's."

"Eating featheries is the new version
of eating crow."

"Hockey is the devil's playground!"

**Hockey fans must learn
to think outside the box!**

**"Don't eat it...
I think it's road kill!"**

Great minds of the world meet...
Can anyone explain the "HIGH FIVE"?

Ice "CAP" ades

**Las Vegas Casino "Cheater"
finally gets a hockey team.**

**"Mr. Pucker, you got to use
your glove hand more."**

**Queen Mother celebrates 200th birthday...
joins a Canadian hockey team.**

Just before the Mongol Herds attack the Frozen North... they played hockey.

Michaelangelo creates "God"...
God creates Hockey

"We only sign players who can read numbers on uniforms!"

Sparky and Slasher both fell on the ice!

"OOG... what's a hockey puck?"

Frosty gets penalized for
"High Checking"

"We can get in another *face off* before it gets here!"

**Bilionaire NHL owner declares
ALL STIR GAME...
Alcatraz vs. San Quentin**

Washington Capitals cross the blue line.

"You'll be fine... just warm-up!"

**"Everyone's favorite sport...
buying sports equipment and goods!"**

"Hockey's world attitude toward sport drugs!"

"Don't be sad... the game is over.
Be happy it happened!"

"I recommend the Stanley Cup to all my patients since delusions give you an excellent cardio workout!"

"He's so slow, it takes him 90 minutes to watch 60 Minutes!"

"Look! I got Stanley's cup!"

**"I got a hockey scholarship,
but that didn't last too long!"**

Robert A. Tiritilli

Award-winning cartoonist, Robert A. Tiritilli—a true sports aficionado—is passionate about all sports and loves to make fun of the pastime and all those who play it. He has drawn 1,000's of different sports cartoons and creates his outlandish style of sports cartooning by combining representative portraiture with cartoonish light-heartedness.

He uses a unique sense of silliness to strike a chord with anyone who plays or enjoys sports, whether they are athletes or couch potatoes.

He finds more ways to blend humorous cartoons with crafty captions. This cartoonist plays with a deck of cards containing every shade of sports humor—wit, satire, jesting, and clowning.

Laugh until your sides hurt with his collections of hilarious sports cartoons! Tiritilli has put the "F" back into the word "FUN."

Sports has more words, terms, and phrases that lend themselves to humorous reinterpretation based on their literal meaning.

The fun of these cartoons at its best is when it shifts the meaning of a sports phrase into another one. But in some cases, the pictures take the obvious joke and make it better with a hilarious execution.

Robert A. Tiritilli

Robert A. Tiritilli is an artist who works in several mediums.
His favorite is the traditional pen & ink technique, which he
has produced thousands of detailed artworks. Recently,
he has created several works of graphic fine art in the
labor-intensive and time-consuming medium of scratchboarding.
Scratchboarding is a drawing technique whereby you scratch
or carve a design on the surface of a black board, revealing white
underneath. It has the opposite effect of drawing with black ink
on white paper. Since it is a reverse drawing method,
it requires learning special techniques to master it,
which Tiritilli did.

www.ingramcontent.com/pod-product-compliance
Lightning Source LLC
Chambersburg PA
CBHW030538130626
46552CB00006B/2324